DEADTIME STORIES™

Welcome to the Terror-Go-Round

A. G. Cascone

Troll

For Uncle Mickey and Johanna,
for riding with us through all of life's little
"Terror-Go-Rounds"

Copyright © 1997 by A. G. Cascone, Inc.

Published by Troll Communications L.L.C.

Deadtime Stories is a trademark of A. G. Cascone, Inc.

Printed in the United States of America.

10 9 8 7 6 5 4 3 2 1

CHAPTER 1

Alex Taylor was on the run.

It was a hot summer evening, and sweat dripped down his face as he tried to escape the monster who had driven him from his own home.

The monster was fast, but not as fast as Alex.

The problem was that Alex didn't know where to find a safe place to hide. So he just kept running.

At the corner of his block, he turned and headed for the old covered bridge that led into the center of town.

On any other day, he would have stopped to pick up a few stones and toss them over the side of the bridge into the little river that ran beneath it. But not today. Today, his only thought was escape.

His feet hit the wooden planks of the bridge hard. The sound of his footsteps echoed off the walls and roof that enclosed him.

He was more than halfway across before he heard a second set of footsteps behind him.

"Why don't you just give up?" the monster bellowed, his voice reverberating.

No way! Alex thought. But he didn't waste his breath saying it out loud. Instead, he used his energy to move his legs even faster.

"You'll never get away from me!"

This time Alex did answer. "Leave me alone, you miserable little monster!" he shouted as he stepped off the other side of the bridge.

He heard laughter behind him as he made the turn onto Main Street.

Alex leaped off the sidewalk and into the gutter just a half-second before he crashed head-on into old Mrs. Wilcox, his next-door neighbor, who was headed home with a bag of groceries.

"Watch where you're going, young man," Mrs. Wilcox admonished.

"Sorry, Mrs. Wilcox," Alex said over his shoulder as he kept right on running.

But Mrs. Wilcox didn't hear him. At that very moment, the old lady let out a scream as the monster missed her by inches.

Of course, the monster didn't bother to apologize to Mrs. Wilcox. He just kept coming after Alex.

"You're not going to get rid of me," the creature called out.

Alex knew that was the truth. He'd been trying to get

rid of the horrible monster for eleven years. But it never worked. It never would. Alex was stuck with him for life.

"Go home!" Alex yelled at his younger brother, Joey. "Leave me alone!"

But Joey hadn't left Alex alone since the day he was born. In fact, Alex and Joey were so close in age and appearance, most people thought they were twins.

Joey was only eleven months younger than Alex, and just a year behind him in school. Shortly after Alex had started to walk, Joey was already learning how to crawl—right under Alex's skin. By the time *Joey* started to walk, there was no way for Alex to escape him.

Still, Alex kept trying.

He ran even faster, dodging other people who were walking along the sidewalk. But Joey kept following, determined to catch up.

Alex turned off Main Street at Schoolhouse Road. He hadn't meant to do it. It must have been force of habit that made him follow the path he'd taken for six years of his life—the path to his old elementary school. Even though he'd already been in middle school for two years, Alex often found himself wandering back to the playground at his old school. There was something comforting about the playground. Alex still liked the swings, and the jungle gym, and the seesaws. The playground was where he went when he wanted to be alone to think, or just to escape.

But there was never any escape for Alex. Wherever he went, his brother was sure to follow.

Alex finally gave up. He plunked himself down in one of the swings and sat there catching his breath as he watched Joey slow his pace to a smug strut.

"Can't you find something better to do with your time than bother me?" Alex groaned as his brother sat down in the swing beside him.

"Not in this crummy little town," Joey complained.

Alex didn't say anything. His brother was right. Middletown was without a doubt the most boring place in the entire world.

Nothing good ever happened in Middletown. Nothing bad ever happened in Middletown. Nothing at all ever happened in Middletown. As far as Alex was concerned, Middletown was the armpit of the universe.

Middletown's only claim to fame was that a Revolutionary War battle had been fought there. There was even a battle monument in the center of town, shaped like a tall obelisk. It was so revered that nothing was allowed to be built higher than the monument just so it could be seen from anywhere in town. In fact, Alex could see the top of it from where he was sitting.

"I hate living in this podunk town," Joey complained. "There's not even anyone fun to play with."

"At least not this week," Alex agreed.

Alex's best friend was away at camp. Joey's best friend was on vacation with his family. So the two of them were stuck with each another. To Alex's way of thinking, that was a fate worse than death.

"So what are we going to do?" Joey asked. "Just hang

around here at this playground like a co

Alex shrugged as he began to rock back
his swing. What else was there to do?

As the two boys sat silently, a strong wind whip
around them. The unoccupied swings started mo   g.
The seesaws went up and down, banging on the ground.

"What's going on?" Alex said, covering his eyes to
protect them from the dirt particles blowing around.

"It looks like a storm is coming," Joey answered. "Look
at the sky."

When Alex glanced up, he couldn't believe his eyes.
He'd never seen clouds as thick and black as the ones
rolling in overhead. Within seconds, the clouds
completely blotted out the rays of the setting sun. The
playground turned as dark as night.

"That is one mean-looking storm," Alex said to his
brother as the wind whipped around them. "We'd better
get home before we get caught in it."

As the two boys hopped off their swings, a deafening
clap of thunder shook the ground beneath their feet. At
the same time, a blinding bolt of lightning hit a tree in
the distance, splitting it right in two.

"Whoa," Joey gasped, staring at the smoking tree.

"Let's get out of here!" Alex cried, grabbing Joey by the
shirt.

Before they'd taken even a couple of steps, though,
there was a huge cloudburst.

But it wasn't rain that fell from the sky.

It was something else, something very, very strange.

CHAPTER

2

Alex and Joey stood frozen on the playground, staring up at the stormy sky.

Not a drop of rain fell on them. Instead, it was as if the clouds had exploded into a shower of confetti. Small bits of colorful paper fluttered all around them.

"What is this stuff?" Alex asked, trying unsuccessfully to snatch it out of the air.

Joey was busy collecting the pieces that had fallen at his feet. "It looks like tickets," he answered.

"Tickets to what?" Alex wondered, gazing in bewilderment into the sky.

Before his very eyes, the clouds simply dissolved. In an instant the sky was as calm and clear as it had been before. The wind had stopped too. And the paper shower was over.

"They're tickets to a carnival!" Joey cried excitedly.

"What?" Alex asked, even more confused. He looked down at the ground and saw that it really was littered with what appeared to be tickets. He bent down to pick one up.

"This is too cool," Joey said as he collected more and more of the tickets.

Alex examined the one he had in his hand. "Arboc's Carnival," he read aloud. "What is that?"

"Duh," Joey answered. "It's a carnival, you moron." He continued snatching up tickets. "Don't you get it?"

Alex looked around at all the tickets that had fallen, then back up at the clear sky. "No," he said nervously. "I don't get it at all."

"It's obvious," Joey told him. "A carnival is coming to town."

"How do you figure?" Alex asked.

"Boy, you really are dumb," Joey said, shaking his head in exasperation. "Where do you think these tickets came from?"

"They dropped out of the sky," Alex reminded him. "Out of nowhere."

Joey laughed. "Not out of nowhere," he said. "That's impossible. There must have been an airplane behind those clouds. Somebody in the airplane dropped the tickets."

Alex began shaking his head. He hadn't seen an airplane, even after the clouds had disappeared. He hadn't heard one either.

"I'm telling you," Joey insisted. "This was some kind of

publicity stunt to advertise the carnival and get people to come. And we lucked out big time, because there's nobody else here but us to collect all these tickets! That means that we'll get to go to the carnival and go on all the rides for free! Is this too cool, or what?"

"It's too weird," Alex replied, dropping the ticket he had in his hand. "If a carnival really is coming to town, how come nobody has heard about it?"

Joey didn't answer. He just kept picking up tickets.

"I don't have a good feeling about this," Alex said.

"You don't have a good feeling about free stuff?" Joey laughed at Alex again. "You really are an idiot."

"I think we should head home," Alex told his brother.

"Not until I get every single one of these tickets," Joey said.

Alex knew it was pointless to argue. When Joey got some hare-brained idea in his head, there was no talking him out of it. Alex was left with two choices. He could go home by himself and tell his parents that he'd left Joey back at the playground—and probably get yelled at. Or he could help Joey gather up the stupid tickets so they could get out of there.

He chose the second option. And he didn't say a word as Joey babbled on about how cool it was that for once there was going to be something fun to do in Middletown.

By the time they'd finished, Joey's pockets were bulging with carnival tickets, and the last rays of the sun were disappearing behind the trees.

"Can we go home now?" Alex asked impatiently.

Joey didn't answer. He just started walking.

Now it was Alex's turn to follow Joey and pester him.

"It must be after eight o'clock," Alex said. "Mom and Dad are going to be furious that we've been gone so long without telling them where we went."

"You were the one who ran out of the house after dinner," Joey reminded him.

"To get away from you," Alex responded.

"Well, I won't be in trouble with Mom and Dad," Joey snickered. "I'll just tell them that I went looking for you."

"You're such a little snot," Alex said, shoving his brother from behind.

"Watch it," Joey warned over his shoulder. "You'd better be nice to me or I won't share my carnival tickets with you."

"Big deal," Alex snorted. He still refused to believe that a carnival was coming to town.

Their parents didn't believe it either, even after Joey showed them the tickets and explained how they'd fallen from the sky. All their mom and dad cared about was that the two boys had left the house without telling anyone where they were going. Just as Alex had predicted, their parents were furious with both of them. They didn't want to hear any crazy stories. Alex and Joey were sent straight to their rooms for the rest of the night.

While that meant no TV, Alex was just as happy to lock himself in his room and read. At least he was away from his brother.

Until about midnight, when Alex was startled from a sound sleep.

"Get up!" Joey whispered in his ear as he shook Alex roughly. "Get up! You've got to see this!"

"How did you get in here?" Alex snarled. He clearly remembered locking his door.

Joey flashed a key in front of his face. But before Alex could steal it away from him, Joey put it back into the pocket of his jeans.

"What are you doing all dressed?" Alex asked, rubbing his eyes.

"We're going out," Joey told him.

"Oh, no, we're not!" Alex said, rolling away from Joey. "You're getting out of here."

Joey plunked himself down on the bed and started tugging at Alex to make him pay attention. "The carnival is coming," he whispered. "Right now!"

"Get away from me," Alex growled, trying to free himself from his brother's grip.

"Just look out the window," Joey insisted.

Alex knew that he wouldn't get another moment's sleep until he did what Joey wanted. So he sat up, pushed his brother out of the way, and got out of bed.

Joey led Alex to the window and pulled up the blinds. "Look!" he said excitedly, pointing outside.

Alex saw immediately what Joey was pointing at. A caravan of wagons was moving down Bridge Street and crossing the covered bridge.

"Didn't I tell you?" Joey gloated.

"I guess you were right," Alex was forced to admit as he watched the caravan move along slowly, one wagon after another disappearing into the bridge.

He should have been excited by the idea of a carnival, especially since they had all those tickets. But something was bothering Alex. There was something freaky about that caravan.

He didn't realize what it was until the last wagon moved onto the bridge. And then it was too late for him to be sure of what he had seen.

But the image was clear in his mind. None of the carnival wagons had drivers.

CHAPTER 3

"Let's go!" Joey said, pulling Alex away from the window.

"Go where?" Alex asked.

"Out to the fairgrounds to watch the carnival set up," Joey said.

"Are you out of your mind?" Alex practically shouted.

"Ssshhh," Joey admonished. "You'll wake Mom and Dad. Then we won't be able to sneak out of the house."

"We are not going to sneak out of the house in the middle of the night to go chasing after that carnival," Alex told his brother sternly.

"Why not?" Joey wanted to know.

"First of all, Mom and Dad would kill us if they caught us running around town after midnight," Alex pointed out. "And secondly, there's something creepy about that carnival. Didn't you notice that nobody was driving those wagons?"

"No, I didn't notice that," Joey told him.

"Well, I did," Alex insisted, even though it sounded completely impossible.

"You're crazy," Joey said. "You must have been imagining things. Or maybe you're just trying to scare me. Well, it's not going to work. I'm going. And if you won't come with me, I'll go alone."

Joey turned and headed for the door.

"Wait a minute," Alex whispered after him. Once again, Joey had him in a bind. Alex didn't want to go anywhere near that carnival. But his parents would kill him if he let Joey go off alone.

Alex knew what he had to do. "I'll go with you," he said. It was the best way to keep Joey out of trouble.

"This is going to be so much fun!" Joey smiled widely, not the least bit surprised to have gotten his own way again.

Alex quickly pulled on a pair of jeans and a T-shirt, then sat down to put on his sneakers.

"Hurry up," Joey said impatiently.

Alex got up and followed his brother out into the hallway. He felt certain he was making a big, big mistake.

The two of them crept silently past their parents' bedroom and down the stairs to the front door. Just as silently, Joey unlocked the door and opened it. Then they both stepped out onto the porch.

While Joey was closing the door, Alex backed into a

stack of paint cans that was sitting on the porch. One can fell over with a loud thud.

"What was that?" Joey hissed, spinning around to see for himself.

The can rolled off the porch. When it hit the ground, the lid popped off and white paint splashed across the lawn.

"Now look what you did." Joey shoved his brother. "I just hope the noise didn't wake up the whole neighborhood."

Just then Alex saw a light go on in an upstairs window of the house next door. "Uh-oh," he whispered. "It looks like old Mrs. Wilcox heard us."

"Let's get out of here before she looks out the window," Joey said, jumping off the porch. "You know how nosy she is."

Joey took off running across the lawn. Alex had no choice but to follow. There was no turning back now. If Mrs. Wilcox came to her window and saw them, she'd definitely call their parents.

Alex watched Mrs. Wilcox's window as he ran. Luckily, the curtains never parted. He was pretty sure they hadn't been seen.

But even if they managed to sneak back into the house without their parents knowing they'd been gone, the boys would still have some explaining to do.

"What are we going to do about the paint all over the lawn?" Alex asked Joey as they headed over the covered bridge.

"Nothing," Joey told him. "The painters get here at the crack of dawn, so Mom and Dad will just think that they spilled it. It's no big deal. Forget about it. We're out to have fun."

As they stepped off the bridge onto Main Street, Alex felt guilty at the rush of excitement that suddenly came over him. It really was cool to be out at night all alone. The streets were quiet and completely deserted. It was like they had the whole town to themselves.

The two boys ran all the way to the end of Main Street, where another road led out to the highway. But Alex and Joey didn't take that road. Instead they simply crossed over to a steep embankment on the other side. The fairgrounds were just on the far side of that hill.

"Let's go," Joey cried enthusiastically as he scrambled up the hill ahead of Alex.

By the time Alex got to the top, Joey was already standing there, staring wide-eyed at the sight below.

The carnival was already up and running.

There was a Ferris wheel, a roller coaster, a merry-go-round, and about a dozen other rides. All of them were already in motion. There were food stands, game stands, and sideshow tents too.

"This is too creepy," Alex said, suddenly feeling nervous again. "How did they get this all together so fast?"

"Who cares?" Joey said as he started down the other side of the hill to get to where the action was.

But even the busy scene looked strange to Alex. Because while there was lots of action, there were no people.

"Joey, please, let's get out of here," Alex hollered, chasing after his brother.

"Get out of here?" Joey repeated incredulously. "You must be kidding. I want to go on the rides. I want to play some games."

"But it doesn't even look like there's anybody here running the place yet," Alex pointed out. "I really think we should leave."

"Forget it!" Joey said emphatically.

They walked between two rows of stands. On one side were all the games. On the other side were lots of good things to eat.

"Cotton candy!" Joey cried, rushing over to a stand that was piled high with the sugary pink treat. He snatched a candy-filled cone off the counter and tore into it.

"You can't just take that," Alex scolded.

"Why not?" Joey asked, stuffing more into his mouth. "There's nobody here to stop me. Besides, it's not like I'm stealing or anything. Some of those tickets say 'good for one free cotton candy.'" He dug into his pocket to find one. "If it will make you happy, I'll leave it on the counter."

Alex couldn't argue with that.

"Here's another one," Joey went on. "Why don't you grab some for yourself? My treat." Joey plunked a second ticket down on the counter.

Alex couldn't resist cotton candy. Still, he hesitated before reaching out and taking a cone for himself.

"So which ride do you want to go on first?" Joey asked.

"I want to go home," Alex insisted.

"Stop being such a baby." Joey laughed at him. He pointed at one of the rides. "There," he said. "That's the perfect ride for you. A merry-go-round shouldn't scare you too much."

But Joey was wrong. As the two of them walked toward the ride, a chill crept up Alex's spine until the hairs on the back of his neck were standing on end.

This was no ordinary merry-go-round. The horses weren't prettily painted ponies. They were huge, wild-eyed, and mean-looking, and they were posed as if they were in the middle of a stampede.

But what bothered Alex most was that the lighted sign over the ride did not read "Merry-Go-Round." The bright neon lights spelled out "Terror-Go-Round." And beneath them, blinking red lights warned, "Ride if you dare!"

CHAPTER 4

As Alex and Joey stepped up to the Terror-Go-Round, the ride came to a sudden stop.

"How did that happen?" Joey asked.

"I don't know," Alex said. "It stopped all by itself." Alex was getting more freaked out by the minute. This whole carnival seemed very strange.

"Maybe it's on a timer," Joey suggested. "Let's get on and see if it starts back up again."

"Why do you want to ride a stupid merry-go-round?" Alex asked, trying to sound indifferent. The truth was, *he* didn't want to ride it.

"Because it's not a merry-go-round," Joey said, smiling mischievously. "It's the Terror-Go-Round. And it says, 'Ride if you dare.' You know I can't pass up a dare." With that, Joey hopped aboard and started checking out the horses. He climbed on the meanest-looking one of all.

"Get on," he told Alex.

"Forget it," Alex shot back.

"What are you, chicken?" Joey taunted.

"No," Alex said, not even convincing himself. "I just think it's stupid, that's all."

"Bawk-bawk-bawk, bawk-bawk," Joey clucked at him.

That did it. There was no way Alex could let Joey make fun of him. His sense of honor overshadowed his good judgment, and he stepped onto the ride to prove he was no coward.

"There," he said to Joey. "Are you happy now?"

"Not until you get on a horse," Joey said, reaching over to pat the one next to him.

Without another word, Alex slid his foot into the metal stirrup and lifted himself into the saddle.

"Now what?" Alex asked. "Are we just going to sit here like a couple of jerks, hoping the ride starts up again?"

"Give it a minute," Joey answered.

They waited a minute. Then two. Then three.

"See," Alex said. "Nothing's happening."

"There's got to be a way to start this thing," Joey insisted, climbing down from his horse. "I'll bet there's a switch somewhere."

As Joey began inspecting the mirrored walls at the center of the ride, Alex climbed off his own horse to follow.

"Here we go," Joey called from the other side of the ride.

Set into the mirrored walls was a glass booth with a

mechanical ticket-taker inside—a man-size dummy wearing a tuxedo and a top hat. Behind him was a blinking sign that read "1997."

The dummy's wooden mouth snapped open. "Tickets, please," he said as Joey stepped up to his window.

Joey dug into his pocket and shuffled through his tickets. He pulled two out of the stack. "'Free ride on the Terror-Go-Round—one way,'" he read aloud before placing them into the dummy's outstretched hand.

The dummy's fingers curled tightly around the tickets as he pulled his hand away. Then he began to laugh maniacally.

The ride did not move.

But the wooden horses did! They all began neighing wildly. Their heads moved up and down, and their hooves pawed at the ground.

"This is too cool!" Joey exclaimed.

But Alex didn't think it was cool at all. In fact, he thought it was scary. He was just about to jump off the ride when it began to spin.

Joey leaped up onto the painted horse nearest him. The horse reared up onto its hind legs, and Joey threw his arms around its neck, holding on for dear life. "This is great!" he shouted to Alex as the mechanical horse continued to buck up and down like a bronco.

Alex wasn't about to get on one of those horses. But as he backed away, the horse behind him wedged its head between Alex's legs and flung him up into the saddle.

Now Alex was the one holding on for dear life. He screamed his head off as the horse galloped beneath him and the ride began to spin faster and faster. If the horse didn't toss him, he was sure the centrifugal force would.

They were moving so quickly that everything outside the ride became one big blur.

Alex was sure he was going to throw up. "How do we stop this thing?" he cried.

"Stop it?" Joey laughed. "I hope it goes on forever. This is even better than a roller coaster."

But the ride didn't go on forever. After just a few minutes of bumping and spinning, the Terror-Go-Round jerked to a halt.

Alex heaved a sigh of relief as he lowered his head and closed his eyes. He was shaking so badly, he knew his legs wouldn't hold him if he tried to climb off the horse. Besides that, his stomach was still in his throat, and he was afraid any movement would only bring it the rest of the way up.

"Alex," Joey said in a quavering voice.

Alex didn't answer. He couldn't.

"Uh, Alex." Joey's voice sounded even more shaky. "Something really weird has happened."

Slowly, Alex raised his head and opened his eyes. He immediately saw the source of Joey's concern.

He squeezed his eyes shut again.

This can't be, he told himself. *It's impossible.*

But when he opened his eyes again, the problem was still there.

It wasn't nighttime anymore. It was the middle of the day. And the carnival was teeming with people—strange-looking people, people who seemed to be from another world.

CHAPTER

5

"Where are we?" Joey asked.

"I don't know." Alex's terrified voice came out barely above a whisper.

The boys climbed off their horses and began looking around at the scene before them.

The carnival itself was the same. But how had it become light outside? Alex was sure that they'd been on the ride for only a couple of minutes, not all night. And where had all the strange-looking people come from?

"I think that, somehow, that ride took us to a different place and time," Alex said nervously to Joey.

"Nope," Joey answered just as nervously. "We're still in Middletown. Look." He pointed toward the hill at the edge of the fairgrounds.

Peeking over the hill was the top of the battle monument.

"We'd better find out what's going on," Alex said, stepping off the Terror-Go-Round.

"How are we going to do that?" Joey asked.

"We'll ask one of these people," Alex told him.

Alex stepped up to a man who was dressed in faded jeans, sandals, a tie-dyed T-shirt, and rose-colored glasses that hid his eyes. He had long, brown, scraggly hair that fell below his shoulders, and an equally scraggly beard.

"Excuse me," Alex said to the man.

But the man didn't answer him. He just walked right past Alex as if he weren't even there.

"That was pretty rude," Joey said, more to the man than to Alex.

"Forget it," Alex told him. The last thing he needed was for Joey to pick a fight with one of these weirdos. "Let's go talk to her." He walked toward a young woman who was dressed in a long, flowing skirt and a billowy blouse. Her waist-length hair was parted in the middle. She had a pleasant-looking face, even though her eyes seemed a little spacey.

"Excuse me," Alex said as he approached her.

She seemed to look right at him for a second. But then another man stepped up beside her and handed her a soda. He wore a beaded headband across his forehead.

"Are you having a good time?" the man asked the woman.

"Yeah," she answered. "This is groovy."

Then the two of them walked away without a glance in Alex's direction.

"Groovy?" Joey said. "What kind of word is that?"

"It's an old-fashioned word," Alex told him. "Back from when Mom and Dad were kids."

"Oh, no," Joey gasped. "You don't think . . ." His anxious voice trailed off as if he were too afraid to finish his question.

He didn't have to finish it. Alex knew exactly what Joey was going to say, because it was what Alex was thinking too. The Terror-Go-Round had sent them back in time. "We've got to find out," he told Joey.

"Hey, mister," he said forcefully to the next man who passed by. "Can you tell me what year it is?"

But the man never broke stride. He didn't even look their way.

"Excuse me, lady," Alex said to an older woman who didn't look quite as strange as the others.

Again, no response.

"What's going on here?" Joey cried. "Are we invisible?"

Suddenly, Alex remembered something. There might be a way to get an answer to their question without having to ask anybody. "Follow me," he told Joey.

"Where are we going?" Joey asked.

"Back to that mechanical ticket-taker," Alex said. "When we got on the ride, there was a sign in his booth that read '1997.' Let's see what it reads now."

Joey followed Alex back to the Terror-Go-Round. They both stepped on and made their way to the ticket window.

Alex's worst fears were realized when he caught sight of the sign inside the booth.

"Nineteen sixty-nine!" Joey yelped. "What do we do now?"

Alex's first instinct was to slug his brother. This was another fine mess Joey had gotten them into. And now that the spit had hit the fan, Joey expected Alex to come up with a plan to get them out of it.

Alex's head was spinning, searching for a solution to their problem. He didn't want to face the obvious answer. But when nothing else occurred to him, he was forced to suggest it to Joey.

"We've got to ride the Terror-Go-Round again." Alex broke the bad news. "Let's hope it takes us back where we belong."

Joey was already shaking his head no. "What if it doesn't?"

"We'll deal with that if it happens," Alex told him. "Besides, even if it takes us somewhere else, we won't be any worse off than we are right now."

"I guess that's true," Joey grudgingly agreed. He dug into his pockets and began searching for the right tickets.

But before he found them, a wooden panel slid down in front of the ticket window. A sign plastered across the panel read, "Closed—Out to Lunch."

"Oh, no," Alex groaned, feeling completely defeated. He stared at the sign in disbelief.

"How can a dummy go out to lunch?" Joey griped.

"Psssst," someone behind Alex hissed in his ear. At the same time, something tickled his neck.

Alex put his hand to his neck as he spun around to see

who was behind him. Immediately his hand went from his neck to his mouth so that he could hold back the scream ready to explode from his throat.

Joey did scream.

But the man in the suit and the bowler hat didn't seem to mind. Nor did he seem surprised by their reactions.

That was completely understandable. He was the most startling-looking man Alex had ever seen.

His shimmering skin was gold and scaly. His eyes were black and beady, with no eyebrows. Instead of a nose, he had a snout with two small nostrils. And his lips were so thin, they were almost nonexistent.

"I sssssssee you got the tickets and decided to accept my invitation to join the show," the strange man hissed.

Alex watched in horror as a forked tongue slithered in and out of the man's mouth as he spoke.

"Who the heck are you?" Joey asked, moving behind Alex.

"I'm Arboc, of course. The ssssssnake-man." He let out a menacing hiss of a laugh. "Welcome to my carnival!"

CHAPTER

6

Alex was almost too terrified to speak to Arboc. But he knew he had to. If anybody could tell him what was going on in this carnival, it was Arboc himself.

"C-can I ask you a q-question?" Alex stuttered.

"Ssssss-certainly," Arboc hissed.

Alex couldn't tell if Arboc was smiling or if the corners of his thin mouth were frozen into a permanent grin. Either way, it was creepy.

"Did the Terror-Go-Round spin us back in time?" Alex asked.

"Clever boy." Arboc sneered. "It's a neat trick, don't you think?"

Before Alex had a chance to answer, Joey piped up. "Yeah," he said. "It's a real neat trick. Why don't you show us how you do it and send us back where we belong?"

"Ah, but you *are* where you belong," Arboc replied, moving closer to them.

"Look, we just want to go home," Joey insisted.

"Before you talk about leaving, there are some people I want you to meet," Arboc told them. "Follow me." He crooked the finger of one of his gloved hands at them, gesturing for them to come along.

Alex and Joey looked at each other, not knowing what to do.

"Do we have a choice?" Alex asked Joey.

But it was Arboc who answered his question. "Not really," he said. Then he began walking away.

Alex and Joey followed obediently.

They made their way through crowds of people who seemed to be enjoying the carnival. As Arboc passed, heads turned and people stared curiously. Some even laughed. But nobody noticed Alex and Joey.

"Hey, Arboc," Joey called, trying to get the snake-man's attention. "Are we invisible, or what?"

Arboc turned his head toward Joey, but he didn't stop walking. "No," he answered, the weird smile still plastered on his face. "You sssssimply do not exist in the carnival. Not yet."

"What's that supposed to mean?" Alex asked.

"We'll discuss it later," Arboc told him, stopping in front of an enormous tent. A sign over the entrance read "Freak Show."

Alex noticed that pictures of the "freaks" were pinned up on the outside wall of the tent to lure people inside.

He couldn't help gawking at the pictures. Joey was doing the same thing.

"I think you're going to like thisssssss," Arboc said, holding open the flap of the tent for them to enter.

Alex went in first, with Joey right on his heels. Arboc followed.

The tent was crowded with onlookers, who were gaping at the freaks, whispering and snickering. They all moved out of the way as Arboc came through.

He began pointing out the exhibits to Alex and Joey. Alex was horrified at the way the freaks were presented, almost like animals in a zoo. But instead of being in a cage, each one was on his or her own little stage with a sign posted in front of it, identifying the person on display.

First there was Bertha the Bearded Lady. She looked at Arboc with fear in her eyes. Then she glanced at Alex and Joey and her expression changed. Alex thought she regarded them with a combination of curiosity and pity.

Alex was surprised that she noticed them at all. But before he had a chance to comment, Arboc moved them along to Sydney the Pig Boy. He was an odd-looking creature indeed—almost as strange as Arboc himself. Though Sydney stood on two legs like a boy, he had the head of a pig. He grunted and oinked like a pig too, much to the crowd's amusement.

Next came Minnie the Fat Lady and Jo-Jo the Midget Man, who was less than half Alex's size.

Next to Jo-Jo, the Rubber Man was busy contorting

himself into all kinds of impossible positions. But he stopped for a moment as Alex and Joey passed by and stared at them.

After the Rubber Man came the Illustrated Man. Every inch of his body was covered with tattoos, even his bald head.

Alex was dumbstruck by the sight of the freaks. Obviously, so was Joey. Why was Arboc showing them these people?

Suddenly, Alex had the horrible feeling that Arboc was really showing Alex and Joey off to the freaks. He looked back and noticed that the freaks seemed to be paying a lot of attention to them. Just as the sideshow customers were whispering and pointing at the freaks, the freaks were whispering and pointing at Alex and Joey.

"How come they can see us when nobody else can?" Joey blurted out.

"You'll sssssssoon find out," Arboc said. "But first meet the newest addition to my carnival. This is Nancy the Dancing Girl." He pointed to the last exhibit, where a normal-looking girl in toe shoes and a tutu spun around and around.

"Why is she supposed to be a freak?" Joey asked.

For the first time since they'd gotten off the Terror-Go-Round, someone other than Arboc spoke to them.

"I can't stop dancing," Nancy wailed pitifully.

"Never?" Alex gasped.

"Never," Nancy cried. "If I were you, I'd get out of here while you still can!"

CHAPTER 7

Arboc just stood there, laughing.

"What do you mean we should get out of here while we still can?" Alex asked Nancy the Dancing Girl.

"Sssssssilence!" Arboc commanded her.

She shot Alex and Joey an apologetic look but refused to say any more. She just went on dancing.

"What did she mean by that?" Joey demanded to know.

"As I told you, Nancy is relatively new to my carnival," Arboc said. "You can't pay any attention to her. She's still upset by the change in her life."

"Listen, dude," Joey snapped, poking Arboc in the chest with his finger. "I don't know who you are, or where you came from, or what you want from us. But I want you to turn that Terror-Go-Round back on so that we can get out of here."

Most people would have thought it took a lot of

confidence for Joey to talk to Arboc like that. But Alex knew that the more Joey tried to act like a tough guy, the more frightened he was. Judging by the tone of Joey's voice, he was terrified.

Alex was just as terrified. He held his breath, waiting for Arboc's reaction.

It certainly wasn't what he'd expected.

"Fine," Arboc said amiably. "If you really want to ride the Terror-Go-Round again, go ahead. You do have more tickets, after all. And I'm quite certain that the ticket-taker is back from lunch now."

"Fine," Joey said. "Let's go," he told Alex as he turned and headed for the exit.

Alex followed him.

"Ride if you dare!" Arboc called after them.

"Maybe we shouldn't," Alex said nervously as they stepped out into the sunlight again. "Maybe the Terror-Go-Round will just take us somewhere else in time."

"Then we'll keep riding it until we get to where we want to be," Joey decided. "What else can we do?"

"Nothing," Alex admitted. If they ever got home alive, he was going to kill Joey for this.

"Hurry up," Joey said, rushing on ahead.

Alex raced to keep up. Then something caught his eye. His feet stopped and he stood staring in disbelief.

"Move it," Joey called over his shoulder.

But Alex couldn't move.

"What is the matter with you?" Joey asked, storming back toward Alex.

Alex just pointed. He hoped he was wrong about what he saw. He hoped that Joey wouldn't recognize the people he was pointing to.

But Joey recognized them immediately, even with their different clothes and hairstyles, and even though they were much younger than Alex and Joey had ever seen them.

"It's Mom and Dad!" he gasped.

CHAPTER
8

"What are Mom and Dad doing here?" Alex cried as he stared at his parents.

"They're so young," Joey said, sounding awestruck.

Their parents *were* young, only teenagers. And they were dressed like all the other teenagers at the carnival, like hippies.

"How come they're not together?" Joey asked Alex.

Their mom was standing with a group of girls who were talking and giggling. Their dad was with a group of guys who were trying to act cool as they ogled the girls.

It took Alex a minute to realize what was going on. Then the truth struck him like a bolt of lightning. It was a story he'd heard ten million times. "They met at a carnival," he reminded Joey.

"Not *this* carnival," Joey declared, shaking his head furiously. "It can't be."

"I'll bet it is," Alex said, moving closer to their mom so he could hear what she was saying to her girlfriends.

"That guy over there is pretty cute," she told them, glancing at their dad.

"Yeah," one of her girlfriends agreed. "And he keeps looking at you."

"Why don't you go talk to him?" another girl suggested.

"I couldn't." Their mom giggled nervously. "What would I say?"

"Well, you'd better think of something," the first girl said. "Because he's on his way over here."

Alex and Joey stepped to one side as their dad walked past them and stopped in front of their mom.

"Hi," he said tentatively.

"Hi," she responded shyly, lowering her eyes as her girlfriends snickered in the background.

Their dad took a sip of the soda he was holding, clearly stumped as to what to say next.

"Um," he started. "I'm Jonathan Taylor."

"Susan Crawford," she answered.

"It's nice to meet you, Susan," their dad said.

"Same here," she replied.

"Why are they acting so geeky?" Joey asked, cringing.

"Because they don't know each other yet," Alex told him curtly. He was more interested in watching what was going on with his parents than in Joey's stupid questions.

"I guess you noticed I was over there looking at you." Their dad gestured back to where he'd been standing with his buddies.

Their mom just smiled.

"My friends bet me I wouldn't have the courage to come over here and talk to you," he went on.

"I'm glad you did," she said, smiling even wider.

Now their dad smiled too. "So maybe you'd like to go on one of the rides with me?" he asked her. "I've got plenty of tickets for everything."

"No!" Joey screamed. "Don't go on any of the rides! They're dangerous!"

But his parents didn't hear him.

"Sure," their mom said happily. "How about that one?" She pointed to the ride that was closest—the Terror-Go-Round.

"Definitely not that one!" Joey cried even more frantically. "Alex, we've got to do something to stop them. We can't let them ride the Terror-Go-Round. Who knows what will happen to them?"

Alex agreed wholeheartedly. But how could they stop their parents? They were already walking toward the ride.

"Mom! Dad!" Alex called frantically as he chased after them. "Please! Try to hear us!"

But their parents were completely oblivious to them. In fact, they were completely oblivious to anything but each other.

Just as they were about to step onto the ride, their mother turned around to smile up at their father again. At exactly the same moment, Joey hit his father's arm—hard. "Dad!" he yelled at the top of his lungs.

Whether their father heard him or not didn't matter. What did matter was that the drink in his hand went flying—right into their mother's face.

She screamed in shock as she stepped back. Then she looked down at her soda-drenched blouse. "Why did you do that?" she shrieked at their father.

"I—I—" he stuttered, confused, looking at the empty cup that was still in his hand.

"You creep!" She slapped him across the face and stormed back to her girlfriends.

"You stupid jerk!" Alex hollered at Joey. This time he didn't stop himself from slugging his brother in the arm. "Now look what you've done. She hates him."

Meanwhile, their father was walking back toward his own friends, looking totally depressed and defeated.

Alex heard laughter coming from behind them as he and Joey watched their parents go off in separate directions. He didn't have to turn around to know whose laughter it was.

"Well, well, well," Arboc sneered as he stepped between the two boys. "You've done a very good job indeed. Now your fates are sealed."

CHAPTER 9

"What should we do?" Joey asked Alex. "Should we go after Mom and Dad and try to get them back together?"

"What good would that do?" Alex answered. "They can't see us and they can't hear us. All we can do is get on that Terror-Go-Round and hope it takes us back where we belong."

"Right," Joey agreed.

Arboc stood listening to them, his forked tongue flicking in and out of his unnerving smile. "Have a nice trip," he said as they stepped onto the ride.

"We will," Joey answered in his best tough-guy voice. Then he stormed up to the ticket window and dug into his pockets to produce his wad of tickets. Once again, he shuffled through them and came up with two "one way" tickets. He slapped them into the ticket-taker's mechanical hand.

But nothing happened. The ticket-taker didn't move. And neither did the Terror-Go-Round.

"I thought you said we could ride this thing," Joey hollered at Arboc.

"You can," he answered.

"Then how come this guy isn't taking my tickets?" Joey asked.

"Perhaps you've given him the wrong ones," Arboc suggested.

"I gave him the same ones I gave him last time," Joey said.

"That's the problem," Arboc told him. "You can't go the same way twice in a row. Besides, I don't think you want to."

Alex couldn't help thinking that Arboc's behavior was awfully fishy. Why was he trying to be so helpful all of a sudden? It could mean only one thing—trouble.

And even more trouble was headed their way.

All the freaks had followed Arboc out of the sideshow tent and were gathering around the Terror-Go-Round, laughing at Alex and Joey.

"What's so funny?" Joey snarled as he looked through his tickets, trying to find the ones that would start the ride.

"You're going nowhere," Sydney the Pig Boy snorted.

"There's nowhere to go," Jo-Jo the Midget Man said.

"Not for you, anyway," Rubber Man told them.

"Not anymore," the Bearded Lady added with a chuckle.

They all seemed to find Alex and Joey's predicament pretty amusing—all except Nancy the Dancing Girl. Alex saw tears glistening in her eyes as she spun around and around in her never-ending ballet. "I hope you can get away," she said. "I hope you don't end up like me."

"Ah-ha!" Joey said, waving two tickets in the air. "These will take us the other way," he told Alex.

"Give them to the dummy," Alex instructed Joey.

As Joey did, Alex glanced sadly back at Nancy.

Once again, the dummy snatched the tickets and laughed.

The ride began to move.

"See you around," Arboc said menacingly.

"Not in this lifetime," Joey assured him with all the bravado he could muster.

"Hurry up and get on a horse," Alex told his brother. Then he climbed onto one of his own, just seconds before the creature sprang to life.

Joey was almost tossed as he clambered into the saddle of the horse next to Alex. Somehow he managed to hang on as they began to spin.

Alex checked the date in the ticket-taker's booth. He watched as "1969" became "1970," then "1971."

Then the horses they were riding passed the booth and Alex couldn't see the date anymore. By the time they made the next pass by the ticket booth, they were already in the late 1980s.

The ride was picking up speed, and the horses were bucking even more violently than they had the last time.

It took all of Alex's strength to hold on.

When they passed the ticket booth again, they were moving so quickly that Alex didn't even catch a glimpse of the date. But he had the terrible feeling that they'd already gone way too far.

CHAPTER

10

The Terror-Go-Round spun around, and around, and around, gaining speed with every turn.

Alex was beginning to believe it would never stop. Or maybe he was hoping it would never stop. Because he was quite certain it was not going to take them where they wanted to go.

When the ride finally did come to a screeching halt, Alex found himself right in front of the ticket booth. As he climbed down from his horse, he looked inside to see the date.

"It's 2525!" he gasped, holding on to the horse so his wobbly legs didn't give out beneath him.

The ticket-taker laughed his hollow, mechanical laugh. Then the panel slid down in front of the window. The ticket booth was closed again.

"Twenty-five twenty-five?" Joey repeated as he got off his own horse. "That's *way* in the future. Everybody we ever knew is probably dead."

But the carnival was even more populated than it had been before.

And while the carnival itself looked just the same, everything else was very different, except for the fact that they were still in Middletown. Alex knew that for sure because he could see the battle monument. It was still the tallest structure in town.

"So this is what Middletown is going to be like in the future," Alex murmured as his eyes scanned the fairgrounds.

"This looks like a scene out of the 'The Jetsons,'" Joey told him.

Joey was right. It did look like a "Jetsons" cartoon, or a science fiction movie.

Alex was so astounded by what he saw that for a moment he almost forgot his fear.

People were flying! Not in airplanes, but all by themselves.

They were dressed in shimmery space suits with little backpacks that propelled them through the air.

Off in the distance, Alex could see miniature spaceships taking off and landing in the parking lot.

"I guess people don't drive cars anymore," Joey said, sounding every bit as amazed as Alex.

"I guess not," Alex agreed numbly.

"This is all pretty cool, actually," Joey decided, stepping off the Terror-Go-Round.

"Where do you think you're going?" Alex hurried after his brother.

"As long as we're here, I want to take a look around," Joey said. "I've always wondered what life would be like in the future. And this is pretty much the way I imagined it."

Alex had always wished he could visit the future too. But now that he was here, all he really wanted to do was go back to his own normal, boring life again.

"I've got to try one of those flying backpacks," Joey declared enthusiastically.

Alex grabbed Joey by the back of the shirt before he could run away. "Oh, no, you don't," he told Joey. "We don't have time to play around. We've got to figure out how to get home."

"We know how to get home," Joey said. "We just have to ride the Terror-Go-Round. Sooner or later it's got to take us back to where we started."

Alex had his doubts about that. But it was the only hope he had to hang on to. "Then we're going to stay right here until that ticket booth opens up again." Alex sat on the edge of the ride and pulled Joey down onto his butt beside him.

"You've got to be kidding me." Joey groaned. "Where's your sense of adventure?"

"It's *your* sense of adventure that keeps getting us in trouble," Alex grumbled. "From now on, we're going to do things my way. Now hand over those tickets."

Joey dug into his pockets and practically threw the

tickets at Alex. "There," he said. "That's all of them."

Alex started flipping through them, looking for the ones that gave them free rides on the Terror-Go-Round. There were tickets for the balloon game, the skeet shoot, and the ring toss, tickets for food and the fortune-teller—tickets for everything. Well, almost everything.

Alex checked through the stack a second time. Then a third.

He gulped hard before breaking the news to Joey. "We've got big problems, pal," he told his brother. "We can't ride the Terror-Go-Round again. We've got no tickets!"

CHAPTER 11

"There have to be more tickets for the Terror-Go-Round," Joey said, snatching the stack out of Alex's hands.

Alex watched as his brother searched through the tickets, only to find out that Alex was right.

"Now you have all the time in the world to check out the future," Alex hollered at Joey. "Because it looks as though we're stuck here for good!"

"Calm down," Joey snapped. "There's got to be a way out of this mess. Just give me a minute to think, and I'm sure I can come up with a plan."

Alex groaned. That was just what he needed, another one of Joey's plans.

It didn't take long for Joey to think of one. "Du-uh," he said, hitting himself on the side of the head. "The answer is simple. We'll just *buy* more tickets."

"Do you have money?" Alex asked hopefully.

Joey hesitated. "No," he answered. "Don't you?"

"No!" Alex replied. "Besides, who knows if they even use the same money anymore?"

"Then we'll have to try to borrow money from somebody." Joey jumped to his feet and rushed over to a family that was standing nearby. "Excuse me, mister," he said to the father.

Alex could have told Joey that he wouldn't get an answer from the man. Even in the future, Alex and Joey didn't exist. Nobody could see them, and nobody could hear them—nobody but Arboc and his sideshow freaks.

As Joey headed back toward Alex, looking defeated, Alex realized what had to be done. "We're going to go find that Arboc guy," he told his brother.

"Why would you want to do that?" Joey asked. "That guy is too creepy. He really scares me."

"He scares me too," Alex admitted. "But this is his carnival. And something tells me he's the only one who knows how to get us home."

"And what makes you think he's going to share that information with us?"

"We're going to have to find a way to get it out of him," Alex decided. He started making his way through the crowds of people who were playing games and buying food. "Keep your eyes open for that snake," he told Joey. His own eyes darted around the carnival.

"Where are you going?" Joey asked as he followed.

"Back to the sideshow tent," Alex told him. "If Arboc's

not there, maybe one of those freaks can tell us where to find him."

"Good thinking," Joey said.

Alex only wished he could say the same thing about any of Joey's ideas.

When Alex got to the entrance of the sideshow tent, he turned to make sure Joey was still with him. But his brother was gone.

"Joey!" Alex called out over the din of the carnival.

There was no answer.

"Joey!" he called again, his eyes searching frantically.

A small group of people was standing just a few feet away from Alex, gawking at the pictures of the sideshow freaks that were posted on the side of the tent. As they moved out of the way, Alex spotted Joey standing there, staring at the pictures.

"Jo-ey!" Alex shouted even louder.

But his brother seemed hypnotized.

Alex stomped over and hit him on the arm. "What's wrong with you?" he growled. "Didn't you hear me calling you?"

Still Joey didn't speak. His eyes were fixed straight ahead and his mouth hung open.

"Why are you looking at those stupid pictures?" Alex asked. "We've already seen them."

"Not this one," Joey said weakly, pointing to the picture that had captured his attention.

At first it didn't make any sense to Alex. It wasn't a photograph, it was a primitive-looking painting. Then he read the notice beneath the picture and his eyes snapped back to the image itself. The likeness was unmistakable. Now Alex understood Joey's reaction.

"'Coming soon.'" Joey read the notice aloud in a voice cracking with fear. "Alex and Joey, the Siamese Twins.'"

CHAPTER 12

"It's the two of us!" Alex cried, staring at the picture in horror.

"It sure looks like us," Joey agreed. "But it can't be us. We're not Siamese twins."

Just as Joey said that, he bumped into Alex, hard.

"Hey!" Alex protested.

Joey kept leaning against him.

"Get off me!" Alex pushed his brother away.

Joey slammed into him again.

"What are you doing?"

Joey pulled himself off Alex. "I'm not doing anything," Joey insisted. "It's happening all by itself. It's like we've got magnets in our pockets."

"That's crazy," Alex told him. But before he'd even gotten the words out, he found himself crashing into Joey.

"See?" Joey said, struggling to pull away from Alex.

They were being drawn together by some strange, unseen force that was making it more and more difficult for them to stay apart.

"We've got to make this stop," Alex said, forcing himself away from Joey and moving toward the entrance to the tent. "Come with me," he told his brother. "But don't get too close."

Joey trailed a safe distance behind as he followed Alex inside.

"Where's Arboc?" Alex roared at the freaks as they performed for their futuristic customers.

"They're ba-ack!" Sydney the Pig Boy chortled.

"Back for good," Rubber Man added.

"Oh, no, we're not," Joey said defiantly, moving toward Rubber Man as if he were going to engage him in a fight.

Alex was between them. "Stay over there," he warned Joey.

But it was too late. Joey had already gotten too close. Before Alex could even try to get out of the way, Joey banged into him again.

"You idiot," Alex hollered at his brother as he tried to push him away.

Joey pushed back.

But this time, they couldn't get away from each other. It was as if their jeans had been sewn together, as if there were four legs in three pant legs.

Alex and Joey fought so hard to get apart, they

toppled to the floor. They continued to struggle, pushing and kicking and rolling around.

The freaks just stood there watching them, amused by their predicament.

"Help us!" Alex begged the freaks.

"There is no help for you," Bertha the Bearded Lady told them.

"You are what you are," Sydney the Pig Boy snorted.

"You're just like the rest of us now," Nancy the Dancing Girl sighed as she twirled endlessly on her stage.

"No!" Alex and Joey screamed at the same time.

"Oh, yes!" Jo-Jo the Midget Man laughed. He got off his little platform and ran toward a curtained-off area right next to Nancy's stage. When he reached the curtain, he jumped high in the air and grabbed on to the cord that dangled in front of it. As Jo-Jo rode the cord back down to the ground, the curtain parted.

Behind it was another small stage with a sign in front of it. The sign read "Alex and Joey, the Siamese Twins."

"Welcome to your future!" Jo-Jo sneered.

CHAPTER
13

Alex refused to believe that he and Joey were stuck—stuck together, or stuck in the carnival. There had to be a way out. And he was determined to find it.

He pushed at Joey with all his might.

Rrrrriiiippppp! The sound tore through the air, echoing off the walls of the tent.

"We're free!" Joey cried as he and Alex finally rolled away from each other.

Alex scrambled to his feet and backed as far away from Joey as he could. He looked down and saw that the leg of his jeans was torn, right up the seam. He and Joey really had been attached.

"Why is this happening to us?" he hollered at the freaks.

"Because you took up the dare and rode the Terror-Go-

Round," Nancy answered. "You never should have done that. *I* never should have done that."

"It's how Arboc got all of us," Bertha the Bearded Lady explained.

"Now you're one of us," Jo-Jo the Midget Man informed them. "You belong to Arboc's Carnival."

"Noooooooo!" Alex and Joey screamed at the same time, backing even farther away from each other.

"I want to go home!" Joey cried.

"You can't," Nancy told them. "Not ever."

"If I could get near you, I'd clobber you for dragging me to this stupid carnival," Alex hollered at Joey. "I told you I had a bad feeling about it."

"Calm down," Sydney the Pig Boy grunted. "It's not such a bad life really."

"You don't have to work all that hard," Rubber Man said, turning himself into a human pretzel.

"You'll always be well fed," Minnie the Fat Lady added.

"You'll get to travel back and forth in time," the Illustrated Man told them.

"You'll live forever," Jo-Jo the Midget Man enthused.

"I don't want to live like this," Alex said. "There's got to be a way out."

"We've got to get back on that Terror-Go-Round," Joey insisted. "We've got to get some money to buy tickets."

"You can't *buy* tickets to the Terror-Go-Round," Jo-Jo said, as if they were stupid. "Arboc sends the tickets to the people he wants for his show. Then, if you ride, you're his forever."

57

"We've got to convince Arboc to let us go," Alex said to Joey.

"Never happen," Sydney snorted.

"He didn't let any of us go," Jo-Jo grumbled.

"But he did give us one chance to win our freedom," Minnie told them.

Alex felt a glimmer of hope. "How?" he asked.

"You play for it," the Illustrated Man said.

"But it's no use, really," Nancy went on. "Arboc's games are impossible."

"And sometimes dangerous," Bertha added.

"It's worth a shot," Joey said.

"It's our *only* shot," Alex told him. "What if we win?" he asked the others.

"Then Arboc uses his golden key to turn on the Terror-Go-Round so that you can ride it wherever you want to go," Jo-Jo explained.

"Arboc has a golden key, huh?" Alex said, more to himself than to anyone else. *We have to find a way to get our hands on it,* he thought. But he didn't dare say it out loud. "Where is Arboc now?" he asked the freaks.

"Probably in his tent," Jo-Jo guessed.

"It's right behind this one," Nancy offered. "Arboc is never very far away."

"Let's go see him right now," Alex said to Joey.

They dashed out of the sideshow tent and around back, keeping their distance from each other.

"Look at the size of this tent!" Joey gasped as he turned the corner several steps behind Alex.

It was twice as big as any of the others.

"Yeah," Alex said. "It looks like old Arboc really knows how to live it up." He stepped up to the flap that was the entrance. "Arboc," he called.

There was no answer.

"Arboc!" Alex called again, louder this time.

Still no answer.

"Let's just go in," Joey suggested.

Alex pushed the flap aside and peeked into the tent. He blinked hard. The place was amazing.

"Is he in there?" Joey asked impatiently.

"No," Alex answered, still staring in disbelief at the sight before him.

"So go in," Joey urged him.

Alex stepped into what looked like a pirate's hideout. The tent was full of treasures—treasures that had obviously been stolen from everyplace in time.

Alex walked farther into the tent, checking out the amazing amount of loot Arboc had managed to accumulate. There were chests full of gold and jewels. There were statues and paintings and furniture.

"Wow!" Joey said as he entered. "Look at all this stuff!" He made his way to the nearest treasure chest and scooped up a handful of gold coins and gems. "We ought to bring some of this home with us!"

Alex's mind snapped back to their purpose for being there. "We've got to *get* home," he reminded Joey—and himself. "Forget about all this stuff. Let's try to find that golden key to the Terror-Go-Round."

"Do you really think it's in here somewhere?" Joey asked.

"It's worth looking for," Alex said. "Especially since Arboc's not around."

The two of them began tearing the place apart, digging into treasure chests, looking inside vases and under furniture.

"Keep your eyes out for Arboc," Alex warned Joey. "We don't want him to catch us doing this."

Alex worked his way over to a huge wicker basket that stood in the corner of the tent. It was big enough for a person to fit inside.

Alex lifted the lid of the wicker basket and dropped it onto the floor beside him. He leaned over to look inside. But just as he did, something leaped out at him.

Alex tried to jump away from it. But he was so startled that he tripped over his own feet and went crashing to the ground.

Pain shot up his spine and through the top of his head like a rocket.

But that wasn't his worst problem.

"Alex! Look out!" Joey screamed in terror.

Alex looked up.

A giant, hooded cobra was slithering up and out of the basket. And the horrible creature was poised to strike!

CHAPTER

14

"Get out of the way!" Joey hollered as the giant cobra hovered above Alex, swaying back and forth.

Alex's brain was screaming the same thing.

But somehow, Alex couldn't make his body move. His eyes were locked onto the cobra's, mesmerized by the creature's cold, glassy stare.

The monstrous snake opened its mouth wide, baring its long, pointed fangs dripping with venom.

Alex knew he was going to die. The snake could strike in the blink of an eye and it would all be over.

"Nooooo!" Joey screamed, darting across the room as if he were trying to make it to home plate. His body slid on the floor as he snatched Alex away from the jaws of death.

The boys toppled over each other in their attempt to

climb to their feet and get out of there. Every time they tried to get up, they ended up sprawled on the floor. Once again, they were stuck together!

Alex was sure the cobra would get them both. He flipped himself over so that he and Joey were sitting side by side and looked frantically toward the basket to see if the snake was coming for them.

But the snake hadn't left the basket. In fact, it was standing straight up and something very strange was happening to it. Its skin stretched and moved as if there were another creature inside struggling to get out.

"What's with that thing?" Joey gasped.

Alex didn't answer. He just kept watching as the snake went through its transformation.

First it puffed up. Then it sprouted arms. Its head got rounder, and its facial features became more human.

In less than a minute, the cobra turned into Arboc, fully dressed in his tuxedo.

"You've interrupted my nap," Arboc said tersely, crossing his arms. He stepped out of the basket and walked toward Alex and Joey until he was standing over them. "This had better be important."

"You bet it's important, Arboc." Joey tried to sound tough.

But once again Alex knew how scared Joey was. He knew because Joey was shaking all over. Since the two of them were still attached, Alex could feel every shiver.

"Well, then." Arboc smiled his thin-lipped smile. "What can I do for you?"

Alex and Joey struggled up onto their feet before Joey answered. "You can send us home."

"Yesssssss," Arboc said. "I *can*. But I don't think I want to. You boys will make an interesting addition to my carnival. I think I'll keep you."

"No, you won't," Joey insisted, trying to pull himself away from Alex.

Alex leaned over to grab a heavy chest that sat on the floor next to him. When he got a firm grip on it, he pulled with all his might and finally broke free from Joey.

"What's the matter?" Arboc chuckled. "Are you boys feeling a little too close for comfort?"

Both boys glared at him without answering.

"Get used to it," Arboc told them. "In a very short time you'll be joined together forever."

"Not necessarily." Alex spoke up. "You have to give us a chance to win our freedom, just like you did with everyone else."

"Ah." Arboc sighed. "I see you've been talking with your new friends in the sideshow. What else did they tell you?"

They'd told Alex and Joey it was impossible to get away. But Alex wasn't about to tell Arboc that. He wasn't about to believe it either. "They said you let them play games to win their freedom," he said.

"Yeah," Joey chimed in. "We're ready to play."

"My, my, my." Arboc smiled and shook his head at Joey. "You certainly are a feisty little fellow. It's going to be so sssssssad to see your spirit broken when you lose."

"We won't lose," Joey insisted. "This time *you're* going to be the loser."

Arboc shrugged. "It hasn't happened yet."

"So are you going to let us play?" Alex asked.

"Ssssss-certainly," Arboc agreed. "I'm ready to take my chances. Are you?"

"Not so fast," Joey said to Arboc. "Before we start, I want to see the golden key that runs the Terror-Go-Round."

"Don't you trust me?" Arboc sneered.

Alex and Joey both grimaced.

"Fine," Arboc said, reaching into the collar of his shirt and pulling out a gold chain from which dangled a large gold skeleton key. "Here's the prize. Now let's see if you can win it."

"What do we have to do?" Alex asked.

Arboc threw back his head and laughed. "That, my friend, is for me to know and you to find out."

CHAPTER 15

"Follow me," Arboc said as he slithered out of his tent.

"Where are we going?" Alex wanted to know.

But Arboc didn't answer him. He kept right on walking.

Alex hung back as Joey took off after Arboc. He didn't want the two of them to get stuck together again.

As he stepped out of the tent, he noticed people casting curious glances in his direction. Did they really see him?

"Hi," he said to a boy dressed in a space suit, who was just about his age.

The boy looked at him nervously. "Hi," he mumbled back. Then he pushed a button on his backpack and flew away.

"How come these people can see us all of a sudden?" Alex shouted to Arboc.

"Because now you're true members of my carnival," Arboc answered without looking back.

"Not yet," Joey reminded him.

"Sssssssoon enough," Arboc said smugly. Then he turned the corner and headed into the sideshow tent. Joey and Alex followed him.

Arboc clapped his scaly hands together, drawing the attention of all the customers inside the tent as well as all the freaks. "The sideshow is closed," he announced. "It will reopen in one hour. At that time there will be an interesting new exhibit." He looked purposefully at Alex and Joey as people began to exit the tent.

"I understand someone here has told our new little friends that I would give them a chance to leave my carnival," Arboc said when the last of the customers had walked out.

All the freaks looked down at the floor nervously. Not one of them said a word.

Arboc let them sweat it out for a minute before he went on. "It's all right," he assured them. "Fair is fair. They do deserve the same chance the rest of you got. If they complete three tasks successfully, I will allow them to go. And just for fun, let's have Nancy choose the first game."

Nancy looked at Arboc in horror. "No!" she cried, shaking her head violently. "I don't want to be responsible for ruining their lives."

"Too bad." Arboc shrugged. "If you don't choose a game in three seconds, I'll choose one. And I can guarantee you that my choice will be very bad for them. At least if you choose, they might stand a chance. One . . ." he began counting.

Alex could almost hear Nancy's brain spinning as fast as her toe shoes.

"Two . . ." Arboc waited. "Three. Time's up."

"The baseball toss," Nancy blurted out. "It's the easiest game I could think of," she explained apologetically to Alex and Joey.

"Very well," Arboc said. "Come along, everyone. The games are about to begin."

Arboc led the group out of the tent. Alex and Joey walked right beside him.

"Don't worry," Nancy said as she danced along between Alex and Joey. "You'll be able to win this game."

"They might be able to win this one," Sydney grumbled from behind. "But who knows what Arboc's got planned for them next?"

Alex remembered that somebody had said Arboc's games could be dangerous. He forced that thought out of his mind. He couldn't worry about what was coming next. He had to stay focused on one task at a time.

Luckily, the first challenge was going to be a piece of cake. Nancy couldn't have chosen a better game than the baseball toss. Alex was captain of his Little League team. He was also their star pitcher.

Joey winked at Alex confidently as the strange parade made its way toward the game booths.

"Here we are," Arboc said as he arrived at the baseball toss. "Who's pitching?"

"I am," Alex responded quickly as he stepped up to the counter beside Arboc. For once in his life, he got no argument from Joey.

The freaks made a semicircle around them to watch.

"In case you don't know, the object of the game is to knock over the milk bottles," Arboc told him.

There were six wooden milk bottles set up on a platform about twenty feet away. They were arranged in a pyramid—three bottles in a row on the bottom, two bottles on top of that, and one more on the very top.

"You can do this," Joey said to cheer Alex on. "No problem."

Arboc took three baseballs from the man who was running the booth and set them down in front of Alex. "Go for it," he said, backing away.

Alex picked up the first baseball. He glanced at Joey for moral support and got a nod and a wink. Then he focused on his target. He took a deep breath, drew back his arm, and let it rip.

The ball traveled through the air so fast, it actually whistled.

Alex held his breath.

The ball hit the pyramid dead center.

For an instant, Alex thought he'd nailed it with one pitch. The top three bottles toppled over easily. It looked as if the bottom three were going too. But they only wobbled for a few seconds before coming to rest exactly as they had been before.

Alex blew out his breath in frustration.

"It's okay," Joey encouraged. "You've still got two balls left."

Alex was going to need them both to get the last three bottles. The way those things were weighted, he figured it would be nearly impossible to get all three of them in one shot.

As Alex was trying to decide which two bottles to go for first, Joey inched his way closer to get a better view.

"We haven't got all day," Arboc snapped, breaking Alex's concentration.

"Back off," Joey growled at Arboc. "You take all the time you need," he said to Alex, moving another step closer.

Unfortunately, it was Joey who should have backed off.

Alex fixed his eyes on the center bottle and the right-hand bottle. He took another deep breath and wound up for the pitch.

An instant before the ball left his hand, Joey crashed into him.

Alex let loose a wild pitch that flew over the top of the bottles, missing them completely.

Behind him, the freaks groaned in dismay.

It had been a valiant effort on Alex's part. But even though he had one pitch left, it looked as though this ball game was over.

CHAPTER

16

"Now look what you've done," Alex hollered at Joey. "We're totally sunk." Alex shook his head in despair.

"Are you ready to concede defeat?" Arboc asked.

Joey grabbed the edge of the counter and wrenched himself free from Alex. Then he stomped over to Arboc until they were practically nose to nose. "No way, you cold-blooded reptile. He deserves a makeup throw for that. There was interference."

"Tough luck," Arboc told him. "No makeup throw. It's do-or-die time."

"You can do it," Joey assured Alex.

"No, I can't," Alex said. "It's nearly impossible."

"But not completely impossible," Nancy called from the sidelines. "You've got to try."

"She's right," Joey agreed. "You're a great pitcher. All you've got to do is concentrate and get the job done."

Alex picked up the last ball. He breathed in and out slowly, trying to banish the fear of failure.

His eyes were fixed on the bottles. He was as ready as he'd ever be. His arm went back.

Then a surge of fear squeezed his heart and he chickened out.

Behind him, Arboc hissed in laughter.

Alex's nerves were shot. There was no way he could pull it together.

He looked at Joey and shook his head apologetically.

"We can't just give up," Joey pleaded with him.

"It looks as though you're going to have to," Arboc snickered. "Unless *you* would like to try and knock over the last three bottles."

Joey started to shake his head. Then he stopped.

Alex saw Joey's eyes light up as the corners of his mouth turned ever so slightly into an impish grin. What was Joey thinking?

"Yeah," Joey said to Arboc. "I'll knock them over."

"You've got to be kidding," Alex protested. Joey couldn't pitch to save his life. And his life—and Alex's— was exactly the stakes here.

Joey didn't waste a single word trying to explain himself. He ran to the counter, put his hands down flat on top of it, and propelled himself over to the other side.

"What do you think you're doing?" Arboc barked at him.

Joey ran up to the remaining bottles and kicked them over. "There," he said proudly. "I knocked them down."

71

"But you cheated," Arboc protested. "You didn't knock them down using a baseball."

"You never said we *had* to use a baseball," Joey gloated. "All you said was that we had to knock all the bottles down. And I've done that. We win."

Arboc was fuming. "We'll put it to a vote," he said. He turned to the freaks. "Let me see a show of hands. Who thinks they won this round?"

Nancy's hand shot into the air.

Arboc hissed at her angrily.

Nonetheless, every other hand went up as well.

"Traitorsssssss," Arboc snarled at them. He turned back to Alex and Joey. "Congratulations. You put one over on me," he said. "But now you're finished. The next game won't be so easy. Follow me."

The group followed as Arboc stormed down the aisle of games, past the Water Balloon Game, the Dart Throw, and the Skeet Shoot, and up to the Test of Strength.

The Test of Strength looked like a ten-foot-tall thermometer with a bell at the top. At the bottom, a metal weight rested on a lever. Alex knew that the point of the game was to hit the other side of the lever with a sledgehammer with enough power to send the weight up the thermometer and ring the bell.

"This should do you in quite nicely." Arboc smiled at Alex and Joey.

The rest of the group let out a collective groan.

"Please give my little friends a demonstration," Arboc said to the man who tended the Test of Strength.

The man was the size of a gorilla. His arms were so thick with muscles that each looked twice the size of his waist.

Alex watched in despair as the gorilla struggled to lift the hammer, then grunted with the effort it took to swing it. The hammer crashed down on the lever, sending the weight all the way up to the top, where it hit the bell with a loud clang.

The gorilla set the hammer down on the ground proudly.

"See how easy it is," Arboc said mockingly. "You have three minutes to ring the bell." He pulled a stopwatch out of his pocket and pushed the button. "Go," he told them.

Alex raced over to the sledgehammer, which stood, handle up, on the ground. He got a good grip and tried to lift it. But he would have had better luck trying to uproot a tree.

Joey rushed to his side to help.

They stuck together immediately. But Alex couldn't worry about that now.

"Get a good grip," he told Joey. He waited as Joey wrapped his fingers tightly around the handle just below his own hands. "Okay," he went on. "Let's go on the count of three. One. Two. Three!"

Both boys grunted loudly as they put all their weight into the effort.

But the head of the hammer barely made it two inches off the ground before it fell back down with a dull thud.

"Two minutes left," Arboc announced.

"We're doomed," Alex said to Joey. "We can't even lift this thing."

Joey didn't bother to protest. Alex was right. There was no way they were going to be able to get that hammer off the ground.

It looked as though Arboc had them beat.

"I have an idea," Joey said, using the weight of the hammer as an anchor to wrench himself free from Alex. "Just stay there," he told his brother.

"What are you going to do?" Alex asked.

"I'm going to ring the bell," Joey told him, stepping up to the lever. He bent his knees and jumped high into the air, landing square on the lever.

Once again, Joey had found a way around Arboc's rules.

Alex and the freaks cheered as the weight moved up the backboard toward the bell.

But it only made it halfway.

Alex sighed in frustration as the weight fell to the ground again.

"One minute." Arboc snickered.

Joey tried again. And again. And again. The results were always the same. He didn't weigh enough to send the weight all the way to the top. "You try," he said frantically to Alex.

Alex put everything he had into the jump. But he didn't do any better than Joey had. And there wasn't enough room on the lever for the two of them to jump together.

"You have thirty seconds left," Arboc gloated. "Then you're all mine. Twenty-nine . . . twenty-eight . . . twenty-seven . . ."

CHAPTER 17

"It's over," Alex groaned. "We're going to be stuck in this carnival for the rest of our lives."

"Unless you can ring that bell in fifteen seconds," Arboc said.

Joey took off running.

"Joey?" Alex called after him. What did he think he was doing?

Then Alex laughed out loud in relief when he saw what Joey was up to. Once again, his brother had come up with a plan.

For the first time in his life, Alex was grateful for Joey's scheming mind.

Joey snatched one of the B-B guns off the counter of the Skeet Shoot, took careful aim, and fired away at the bell.

Clang! Clang! Clang! Clang!

The bell rang repeatedly as Joey pelted it with B-Bs from his gun.

The freaks clapped their hands and laughed in delight as Arboc had another hissy fit.

Joey stopped firing and blew on the barrel of the gun as if he were a cowboy at the O. K. Corral. Then he stuffed it into his pocket and strutted over to Arboc. "We win again," he smirked.

"Enjoy your victory, little man," Arboc said. "You may have won *this* battle, but you haven't won the war. And I promise you, you won't." Then he grabbed Nancy the Dancing Girl by the arm. "Since you chose their first task," he hissed in her face, "you can assist them in their last."

Arboc started off, with Nancy twirling along beside him. "Let's see how crafty you are this time," Arboc said over his shoulder as Alex and Joey followed with the others.

Arboc stopped at one of the food stands and grabbed a candy apple off the counter. Then he kept going, holding the apple in one hand and Nancy's arm in the other.

Alex wondered why Arboc had taken the apple. But he didn't dare ask.

They walked past the other games and food stands and rides to an open field, where there was an archery range. Arboc let go of Nancy to take a bow and three arrows from the man in charge. He thrust them into Alex's hands.

"Now listen carefully," he said to Alex and Joey. "This time I will be very specific about the rules so there can be no more cheating. You will have three arrows. You must shoot them from the bow. You will stand fifty paces away from your target. All you have to do is hit the target once and you win. But if you miss the target, the results will be fatal."

"What's that supposed to mean?" Joey demanded.

Arboc pulled the stick out of the candy apple and tossed it onto the ground. "This is your target," he told them, holding out the apple.

"You've got to be kidding," Alex said.

"No, I'm deadly serious," Arboc replied. "And just to make the game more interesting, you will have to shoot the apple off Nancy's head." He pushed the sticky apple down on Nancy's hair as she danced beside him. It stuck firmly. "Let's see how you do with a moving target."

"No way!" Alex told him. "We're not playing." He threw the bow and arrows down on the ground.

"Then it's over," Arboc declared triumphantly. "You're all mine."

"No!" Nancy protested. "You have to try," she begged Alex and Joey.

"Forget it," Alex said. "We're not going to shoot arrows at you. Don't you understand what could happen?"

"I don't care," Nancy told him. "It doesn't matter what happens to me. My life here is worthless anyway. But you have to try to save yourselves."

"What a generous girl," Arboc said, mocking her. "It will

be a pity to lose you." He grabbed her arm again and spun her out into the field, counting paces as he went.

"What are we going to do?" Joey asked Alex.

"I don't know," Alex answered. "We can't shoot arrows at a person."

"Well, we can't stay in this carnival forever either," Joey said. "There's got to be a way to win this game, the way we won the other two."

If there was, Alex hoped it would come to one of them quickly. Time was running out.

CHAPTER 18

"Let's not take all day," Arboc said as he left Nancy alone in the middle of the target range and headed back toward Alex and Joey.

"I can't do it," Alex told Joey, ready to concede defeat.

"Then I will," Joey said, grabbing the bow and one of the arrows that lay on the ground at Alex's feet.

There was no doubt in Alex's mind that Joey was bold enough to try to shoot the apple off Nancy's head. There was also no doubt in his mind that Joey would miss. He couldn't allow his brother to shoot Nancy by accident. But there was only one way to stop him.

"No, I'll do it," Alex insisted, ripping the bow out of Joey's hand. He took the arrow too. But he didn't load it into the bow. He just stood there watching Nancy dance.

"If you're going to do it, do it now," Arboc ordered him.

"Do it," Nancy urged Alex, closing her eyes tightly as she kept on dancing.

"Can't you at least stand still for a minute?" Alex called to her.

"No," Nancy answered. "It's impossible for me to stop dancing."

"I'm waiting," Arboc said impatiently.

Alex loaded the arrow and pulled back on the bowstring, struggling to take careful aim. Maybe he would get lucky. Maybe he could pull it off. But maybe . . .

His brain wouldn't even finish the sentence. It was too awful to think about.

Alex didn't have the nerve to let the arrow go.

"If that arrow doesn't fly by the time I count to ten, the game is over," Arboc declared. "One . . . two . . . three . . ."

Alex's hands were shaking uncontrollably.

"You have to shoot," Joey said as Arboc continued to count.

"Six . . . seven . . . eight . . ."

It was almost over.

Alex had to buy some time. So he shot the arrow. But he shot it into the ground just a few feet in front of him.

"No," Joey groaned, covering his face with his hands.

"One down, two to go," Arboc said smugly as the freaks began to whisper among themselves.

Arboc picked up the second arrow from the ground and held it out to Alex. "Let's get this over with quickly, shall we?" he said. "I'm getting bored."

Alex reached out—but not for the arrow. Instead, he

made a grab for the golden key that hung around Arboc's neck.

He almost got it. The key was in his grasp. His fingers closed around it.

But then Arboc's scaly hand shot up and grabbed Alex's wrist. "Let go," he growled, squeezing Alex's arm so tightly that Alex was afraid his bones would be crushed.

Slowly, reluctantly, Alex opened his hand and let go of the key.

Arboc did not let go. He continued to put the squeeze on Alex. "That little stunt is going to cost you," he said. "You just forfeited one shot. This is your last arrow." He slapped the arrow into Alex's hand in place of the key, then released his grip.

Alex looked at Joey in despair. He was ready to give up now.

But Joey was not. "Get out of the way," he said to Alex, drawing the B-B gun from the Skeet Shoot out of his pocket.

"What are you doing?" Alex cried, jumping back.

Joey didn't tell him. He showed him. He pulled the trigger of the B-B gun and started blasting away at Arboc's feet. "Dance, sucker," he snarled at Arboc as round after round hit its mark.

Arboc *did* dance—more frenetically than Nancy. All the while he was yowling in pain.

He continued to dance, hopping on one foot as he rubbed the other, even after Joey stopped pelting him with B-Bs.

Joey took the opportunity to snatch the key, breaking the chain it hung on as he ripped it from around Arboc's neck.

"You miserable little brat!" Arboc hollered. "You're dead meat!"

"Let's get out of here!" Joey cried.

But before anybody could make a move, Arboc fell to the ground and transformed himself back into a cobra— a cobra ready to strike.

CHAPTER 19

Alex didn't have time to think. He acted on impulse alone.

Just as the cobra reared up, spreading its hood and baring its fangs, Alex shot his last arrow.

He didn't shoot it at Nancy. He shot it at the cobra.

Alex discovered that he was a better marksman than he ever imagined. The arrow went right through the cobra's middle and stuck fast into the ground, pinning the monstrous reptile to the spot.

Joey scrambled out of the cobra's reach as it made one desperate attempt to strike him. "I've got the key!" Joey cried triumphantly, holding it up for Alex to see.

The cobra flailed around, hissing fiercely as it tried to pull free of the arrow.

Joey did a little victory dance right in front of the

snake. "We won! We won!" Joey gloated, wiggling his butt at the creature.

"We haven't won yet," Alex snapped at him. "We're still stuck in this stinking carnival." *And we still have to ride the Terror-Go-Round again,* he thought with a shiver.

"Let's go home!" Joey whooped.

But as Joey took off running, Jo-Jo the Midget Man jumped on his leg and knocked him to the ground. "You're not going anywhere," he said.

"Get off me, you little freak!" Joey yelled, shaking his leg to try and get rid of Jo-Jo.

But Jo-Jo hung on. "No way!" he said. "If you're leaving the carnival, we're coming with you."

All the other freaks muttered in agreement as Nancy danced over to join the group.

"Forget it," Joey told them. "We're not bringing you home with us."

"Who wants to go home with you?" Sydney the Pig Boy snorted.

"We want to go back to our own homes," Bertha the Bearded Lady explained. "With the golden key, you can take us anywhere."

"Fine," Alex agreed. "Let's just get out of here now while we can." The giant cobra was still trying to free itself. And Alex worried that it just might succeed at any moment. "Move it!" he told them all.

Without another word, they began to run, leaving the cobra impaled on the arrow.

Alex led the group out of the field and back toward the games and rides.

The main area was still lively. Futuristic people were enjoying themselves, unaware of the horrors of the carnival.

Alex, Joey, and the freaks ignored the stares and whispers they got as they ran to the Terror-Go-Round.

Alex leaped aboard first, followed by Joey. "Give me the key," Alex said, holding out his hand.

As Joey moved to turn it over, he slammed into Alex—and stuck.

"Not again," Joey cried, trying unsuccessfully to pull free.

"Forget about that for now. Let's just get this ride moving," Alex told his brother. "If we can get out of here, the problem will disappear all by itself."

"If we can get out of here, we'll all be back to our old selves again," Nancy said. "I'll finally be able to stop dancing."

"Does anybody know how to work this thing?" Alex asked the group.

"There's a control panel right under the ticket booth," Bertha told them.

"Yeah," Sydney grunted. "The key fits into that."

Alex and Joey maneuvered their way awkwardly between the horses to get to the ticket booth. Alex spotted a keyhole in the panel just under the window. When he put Arboc's key in and turned it, the panel fell open. Inside were about two dozen lighted buttons.

"What am I supposed to do now?" he asked the freaks as the last of them climbed onto the Terror-Go-Round.

"We don't know," Jo-Jo answered.

"Arboc punches in some kind of code," Nancy told them. "But he's always made sure that nobody can see what it is."

Alex looked at the buttons in front of him. Each one was marked with a symbol. But the symbols made no sense at all to Alex.

"Maybe we should just start pushing buttons and see what happens," Joey suggested.

Alex shook his head. Pushing buttons randomly might get them into even bigger trouble. "Give me a minute to think," Alex said.

But Alex didn't have a minute to think.

Hysterical screaming broke out in the distance.

When Alex turned toward the sound, he saw people running. It looked like a stampede.

"What's going on?" Joey asked, wrenching himself free of Alex.

The answer came as the carnival customers cleared out.

Alex saw the cause of the panic and began to panic himself.

The giant cobra was slithering toward the Terror-Go-Round at lightning speed.

CHAPTER
20

"Do something," Joey yelled.

Alex started pushing control buttons frantically, but nothing happened.

He glanced over his shoulder to see the cobra coming dangerously close. If he didn't get the ride moving, they were all dead.

"Hurry up," Nancy shrieked.

But it was already too late. There was a loud hiss. Everyone screamed as the giant cobra rose up on its coiled tail beside the Terror-Go-Round.

In one last desperate attempt to save them all, Alex spread his hands and slammed them down on the control panel, hitting every button at once.

To his astonishment, the horses sprang to life just as the cobra sprang into the air. The Terror-Go-Round began to spin.

"Hooray!" the freaks cheered, hanging on to the brass poles as the horses began bucking.

"We're going home!" Joey exclaimed, holding up his hand for Alex to high-five him.

But Alex didn't slap Joey's hand. It wasn't time to celebrate just yet. He was afraid the cobra had jumped onto the ride at the last second.

His eyes darted around anxiously. "What happened to Arboc?" he asked the others.

"We left him behind," Sydney squealed in delight.

"Are you sure?" Alex demanded. "Nobody saw him jump on?"

They all shook their heads no.

"Forget about Arboc," Joey said. "We've got to figure out how to stop the ride at the right time."

Joey was right. As the ride spun around and around, the date inside the ticket booth kept changing, moving backward in time.

"At least we're going in the right direction," Alex said. "There's got to be a way to stop this thing."

He tried all the buttons, again to no avail. The years kept ticking away, getting closer and closer to the twentieth century.

"We're going to have to jump off," Joey told Alex.

"No way!" Alex said, still trying his luck with the buttons.

"It's the *only* way," Joey insisted.

"And what happens if we jump off and we're not in the right place?" Alex asked. "Or if something else is wrong? We won't be able to get back onto the Terror-Go-Round and fix it. No," he told Joey, shaking his head adamantly. "We don't get off this thing until it stops."

"I guess you're right," Joey conceded. He started pushing buttons with Alex, trying to figure out how to get control of the Terror-Go-Round.

As the two of them worked on the controls, the date hit the year 2000.

"We're almost there," Joey said, desperately pushing buttons.

"Please stop," Alex cried, pounding on all the buttons at once, just as he had before.

But this time it didn't do any good. The Terror-Go-Round passed 1997 and kept on going.

The freaks started to freak out.

"What are you two doing?" Jo-Jo hollered at them.

"We're not going to be able to get off, are we?" Minnie wailed.

"We're doomed," Sydney grunted.

"Not me," Nancy said. "I'm jumping."

"Don't do it," Alex pleaded with her. "It's a bad idea."

"I don't care," Nancy answered, stepping up to the edge of the ride.

The Terror-Go-Round was spinning so fast that everything outside was a blur.

"You can't even see where you're going," Bertha said.

"It doesn't matter," Nancy told her. "When my number is up, I'm out of here. Anything is better than being stuck in Arboc's carnival." She hung on to the brass pole as her feet danced beneath her. Her body was poised to jump while her head was turned toward the ticket booth, watching time fly.

They passed through 1960 in a flash. Then 1959 . . . 1958 . . .

"There's got to be a better way," Alex insisted.

When they hit 1955, Nancy let go of the pole. "Good-bye, everybody," she hollered as she leaped off the Terror-Go-Round.

For a split second, it was as if they were frozen in time.

Alex caught a quick glimpse of the world beyond the Terror-Go-Round. The carnival was still there. But it did seem to be the 1950s. It looked as though Nancy really had made it home.

Then it was all a blur again.

"She did it," Jo-Jo gasped.

"I'm next," Sydney said, stepping up to the edge as Nancy had done. In 1936, Sydney jumped too.

One by one, all the freaks jumped to freedom.

Bertha was the last to go. "I hope you boys find your way home," she said before leaping off the ride in 1864.

Alex and Joey were all alone.

"We should have jumped too." For the first time in his life, Joey got to be the one to say *I told you so!*

This time it wasn't Joey's impetuous behavior that had gotten them into trouble. It was Alex's caution.

"I'm sorry," Alex said—and meant it.

The year hit zero and kept right on going backward.

"Where are we going?" Joey asked hopelessly. "What's going to happen to us now?"

CHAPTER 21

Where was the Terror-Go-Round taking them? Back to the beginning of time? Back before time began? Back to nothingness?

Alex had to find a way to make the ride change direction. He had to break the code on the control panel. He only hoped he had enough time to do it.

He worked furiously at his task, trying one sequence of buttons after another. Nothing was helping. He glanced over his shoulder to see Joey standing dangerously close to the edge, holding on to a brass pole. "Get away from there!" he hollered to Joey.

Joey didn't move. He just kept staring out into the blur of the world passing them by.

Alex left the control panel to go get him. "Come here," he said, grabbing Joey's arm to pull him back.

Suddenly, something dropped from the roof above.

Both Alex and Joey screamed in horror when they saw what was dangling in front of their faces.

The cobra *had* made it onto the ride. They just hadn't seen him before because he'd been hiding on top.

The two boys scrambled out of the way as the snake opened its mouth and spit a stream of venom that missed them by only inches.

Then the cobra began to wind itself around the pole Joey had been hanging on to. It slithered down to the platform.

There was no escape now. If they jumped off the ride, they were doomed. If they stayed, they were dead.

Alex's eyes were glued to the cobra, watching to see which way it would move, wondering how long they could avoid its inevitable bite.

When the cobra reached the platform, it coiled up, then raised its head until it was almost standing straight up on its tail.

Alex got ready to run the moment the snake moved to strike.

But it didn't strike. Instead, the cobra transformed into Arboc. "I hope you enjoyed your little adventure," he said. "Too bad it was all for naught."

Alex lowered his head in defeat.

But Joey was still brazen. "At least the others got away," he told Arboc.

"Not for long," Arboc snickered. "As soon as I get this ride under control, we'll go back and get them."

"Oh, no, you won't," Alex said, slamming the control

panel shut. He locked it quickly and put the key in his pocket.

Arboc didn't seem terribly flustered by Alex's actions. In fact, he chuckled. "What do you think you're going to accomplish?" he asked with a sneer. "I'm the only one who can control the Terror-Go-Round. If you don't hand over the key, we'll keep riding forever."

"Don't give it to him," Joey said.

Alex had no intention of handing over that key. As long as it was in Alex's possession, the others were safe. And there was still a chance for him and Joey to find a way out of this mess.

If Arboc got the key back, all hope was lost.

Alex and Arboc stood glaring at each other for a long time.

Finally Arboc broke the silence. "I'm really getting quite bored with your shenanigans," he said as he started walking slowly and purposefully toward the boys. "If you don't give me that key right now, I promise you will pay dearly for your lack of good judgment." He held out his hand, waiting.

"Forget it, snake-breath," Joey snarled. "The only way you're getting that key is over our dead bodies."

"That can be arranged," Arboc threatened. He lunged for Alex.

But Alex dodged him. He and Joey took off running.

Arboc followed. "It's useless to run," he hollered after them. "There's no place for you to go."

Alex knew that was the truth. But he wasn't ready to

give up yet. Instead, he and Joey picked up speed, shooting way ahead of Arboc.

That was a mistake.

Arboc doubled around and headed them off at the pass. Before Alex could turn to run the other way, Arboc had grabbed him. "Give me the key," he hissed.

"Never!" Alex said, struggling to break free.

Arboc reached for Alex's pocket.

Alex took the opportunity to knock Arboc off balance. He fell to the floor. But he took Alex down with him.

"Let go of my brother," Joey cried. He tugged at Arboc from behind.

Alex managed to roll out of Arboc's grip. He tried to get to his feet.

But Arboc shook Joey off easily and grabbed hold of Alex before he could stand up. The two of them rolled around and around, struggling desperately.

Before Alex saw it coming, they were at the edge of the ride.

Alex managed to grasp a brass pole to save himself from being tossed over the side.

Arboc wasn't so lucky.

"Aaaaaaggggggghhhhhhh!" he screamed as he flew over Alex's head into the blur.

Time stopped, just as it had when the others had jumped off the Terror-Go-Round.

The world outside was one giant, shimmering mass of ice.

Alex watched as Arboc hurtled through the air, turning

back into a cobra as he went. Then he crashed into a wall of ice, froze solid, and shattered into thousands of little pieces.

Alex was about to cheer—until he realized that the Terror-Go-Round had stopped dead.

CHAPTER 22

"We're going to freeze to death!" Joey cried, shivering from the cold.

Alex was shivering too. He'd never felt such frigid temperatures in his entire life. His breath came out in icy crystals. And when he breathed in, the frostbitten air burned his lungs.

"We must be back in the Ice Age," he told Joey, wondering how long they could survive in conditions that had wiped out all life on the planet.

"Get us out of here!" Joey demanded.

Alex got the key out of his pocket and headed over to the control panel. He had trouble getting the key into its hole, which was already encrusted with ice. The mechanism inside was frozen too. Alex had to jiggle the key until he was finally able to turn the lock.

But then he couldn't get the panel to open.

"Help me out here," he said to Joey as he tried to pry the front of the panel off with numb fingers.

The two of them together still couldn't make the thing budge. It seemed to be frozen solid.

Alex wondered how long it would be before he and Joey were frozen solid too. Their chances of getting out of this mess were becoming bleaker by the second.

"It's moving," Joey announced.

Alex tugged harder on the panel until finally it gave. He knew there was no time to fool around. He slammed all the buttons at once, as hard as he could.

The Terror-Go-Round lurched forward, then stalled.

Alex hit the panel again. His hands were so cold, he was afraid they would shatter the way Arboc had.

The ride lurched again. Then the horses came to life and the Terror-Go-Round began to spin.

"You did it!" Joey said. "We're moving."

"Yeah," Alex sighed. "But in which direction?"

He looked up at the date. It was 10,000 B.C.

Alex closed his eyes for a second, afraid to see which way the numbers would change.

"We're going back to the future!" Joey told him.

Alex leaned against the ticket booth and heaved a sigh of relief. Maybe their long nightmare was coming to an end.

As the ride continued to spin, the air around them warmed up.

"It's too bad we can't figure out how to make this thing

work the right way," Joey said. "Imagine how cool it would be to travel anywhere in time that you wanted to go."

Joey was back to his old self. His mind was already ticking away with new schemes—ticking like a time bomb.

Alex didn't want to hear it. "I think we've had enough time travel, thanks to you," he said. "Do me a favor. Next time you want to go on some wild adventure, leave me out. Okay?"

"You're such a wimp," Joey teased. "Come on, you've got to admit, this has all been pretty exciting."

"It's not over yet," Alex reminded him. "We're still not home free."

"We will be in a couple of minutes," Joey said. "All we've got to do is watch the date and jump off at the right time, just like everybody else did."

Alex looked at the date. They were almost back to the year 1.

"What do you suppose will happen to the Terror-Go-Round once we jump off?" he asked Joey.

Joey shrugged. "I guess it will just keep spinning forever."

Alex continued to watch the date change in silence until they got to the twentieth century. "Let's get ready to go," he said to Joey.

They made their way between the bucking horses to the edge of the ride. "Hold on to my hand," Alex instructed Joey. "I want to make sure we both end up in the same place."

They clasped hands and held on to each other tightly.

When the date read 1990, Alex began counting out loud. "Nineteen ninety-one, 1992, 1993, 1994, 1995, 1996. Jump!"

Alex closed his eyes as he and Joey leaped off the Terror-Go-Round. He was still holding on to Joey's hand as they hit the ground and began to tumble.

When Alex finally got his bearings, the first thing he saw was that the carnival was still there, and so was the Terror-Go-Round. But there were no people.

"Something went wrong," he said to Joey.

"It sure did," Joey agreed. "Not only is Arboc's Carnival still here, it's not nighttime. It was nighttime when we left."

Joey was right. When they'd first gotten on the Terror-Go-Round it was late at night. Now it was early morning. The sun was just beginning to rise. Maybe that was okay. Maybe the night had passed while they were away.

"The good news is we're in Middletown," Joey went on.

Alex looked around and caught sight of the battle monument. At least they were in the right place. But were they in the right time?

Alex was almost too afraid to look into the ticket booth for the answer.

Joey beat him to it. "It's 1997!" he shouted with glee. "We made it. We're home!"

CHAPTER 23

"Why is the carnival still here?" Alex wondered aloud.

"Who knows?" Joey responded. "And who cares!"

"Yeah," Alex agreed. "Let's go home."

They walked through the deserted carnival toward the hill at the edge of the fairground, then down the hill into town.

The town was as empty and still as it had been the night before. It was way too early in the morning for the shops to be open or for people to be out and about.

"Do you think we can make it back into the house without Mom and Dad finding out we were gone?" Joey asked.

"Maybe," Alex answered. "If we're lucky, they won't be awake yet."

Alex knew that was a long shot. His mother was always out of bed at the crack of dawn. The best he could hope for was that she hadn't looked in their rooms and found them missing.

"Well, if they are awake, we'll just tell them we got up even earlier than they did and decided to go for a walk," Joey said. His scheming never ended.

"I don't think they're going to believe that," Alex told him. "Especially since we're wearing the same clothes we had on yesterday." He didn't mention that the last thing in the world he would do of his own free will was take an early-morning walk with his pain-in-the-butt little brother.

"If they find out we were out all night, we'll be grounded for the rest of our lives," Alex said.

"Don't worry about it," Joey reassured him as they stepped onto the covered bridge, nearly home. "If we could deal with Arboc, we can certainly deal with Mom and Dad."

Alex wasn't so sure about that. When his mom was really angry, she was even scarier than a cobra.

"Just remember," Joey went on as they crossed the bridge, "whatever you do, don't act guilty. If you act guilty, then they'll believe we *are* guilty. But if you act innocent and stick to the story no matter what, we'll make out okay."

Joey sounded like the voice of experience. That's because he was. Joey had had to talk himself out of trouble so many times, he was really good at it by now.

Alex just hoped he could work his magic once more. He figured they'd already been punished enough for sneaking out of the house.

"I just want to get back to my room, get into bed, and sleep all day," Alex said as they stepped off the bridge and headed toward the corner of their own street.

"Me too," Joey agreed, picking up his pace and moving ahead of Alex.

By the time they'd turned the corner onto their own street, Joey was pretty far ahead of Alex—too far ahead for Alex to stop him when he spotted trouble.

Joey didn't seem to notice the problem. He kept walking toward it as if nothing were wrong.

Alex rushed after Joey and grabbed him by the back of the T-shirt, hoping there was still time to avoid disaster. "We've got to hide," Alex whispered frantically in Joey's ear, "before old Mrs. Wilcox sees us."

Their neighbor Mrs. Wilcox was dragging her garbage can down her driveway, out to the curb for pickup.

"It's too late to hide," Joey told Alex. "The only thing for us to do is keep walking and act cool."

Alex didn't feel very cool. In fact, he was sweating.

"Hi, Mrs. Wilcox," Joey called as Mrs. Wilcox set the garbage can on the curb. They were less than ten feet away from her.

Mrs. Wilcox didn't answer. She didn't even cast a glance in their direction. She simply turned back toward her house and started walking up the driveway.

"What's the matter with her?" Joey asked Alex.

Alex shrugged, watching Mrs. Wilcox disappear into her house. He didn't know why she'd ignored them, but he was relieved that she had. Maybe she wouldn't say anything to their parents about having seen them.

He was so focused on Mrs. Wilcox that he never noticed the difference in his own house until Joey pointed it out.

"Why is our house blue?" Joey murmured curiously.

Alex blinked hard to make sure he was seeing correctly. "Last night when we left, it was yellow," Alex said nervously. "And all the cans of paint that were stacked up on the porch were full of white paint. Mom was having the house painted white, not blue."

"And where are all the paint cans now?" Joey went on.

There were no paint cans anywhere to be seen.

"We'd better find out what's going on," Alex said, racing for the house. He ran up onto the porch and burst through the door, with Joey right behind him.

Just as Alex had predicted, their mother was already up and dressed, and busy making breakfast in the kitchen. Alex heard her singing to herself happily. He put a finger to his lips to tell Joey to stay quiet. Then they inched their way toward the kitchen to peek in.

At first glance, everything seemed perfectly normal. Alex and Joey watched as their mother carried a plate full of pancakes over to their father, who was sitting at the table with his nose buried in the newspaper.

"Thank you, honey," he said in a very strange voice.

Alex and Joey exchanged confused looks. Then they

turned their attention back to what was going on in the kitchen.

Their father folded up his newspaper and gave their mother a kiss.

Both Alex and Joey screamed at the sight.

The man who had been hidden behind the newspaper, the man they had thought was their father, wasn't their father at all. He was their mailman.

"What's Mr. Kelly doing in our kitchen?" Joey cried.

"And what's he doing kissing Mom?" Alex demanded, totally appalled.

"Happy anniversary," Mr. Kelly said to their mom.

"Twenty happy years today," their mom replied, smiling at Mr. Kelly.

"I can't believe we've been married that long," he told her, smiling back.

"Married?" Alex and Joey shrieked at the same time.

"And all because we met at that carnival," their mom said.

"All because some creep threw his drink in your face," Mr. Kelly added. "I wonder whatever happened to that poor guy?"

"Who cares?" Their mom laughed. "He was a jerk."

"That's Dad she's talking about," Joey said, sounding insulted.

It finally dawned on Alex what was going on. "This is all your fault," he told Joey. "When we rode the Terror-Go-Round back to the day Mom and Dad met, you made Dad throw his drink all over Mom. Because of you, they never got together and got married."

"What are you saying?" Joey was starting to panic. "Mr. Kelly, the mailman, is our dad?"

"That can't be," Alex groaned.

And he was right.

"Good morning, Mom. Good morning, Dad," two boys said as they walked past Alex and Joey and into the kitchen.

"Good morning, kids." Their mom and Mr. Kelly smiled at the two boys who were not Alex and Joey.

"Mom!" Alex screamed, stomping into the kitchen.

She didn't respond. She didn't even look at him.

"Mom!" Joey echoed, pushing past Alex and standing right next to his mother.

She didn't look at him either. She was too busy getting breakfast for her other two children.

"We don't exist," Alex cried. "Because of you, Mom married Mr. Kelly instead of Dad, and they had two kids of their own. Now nobody can see us. That's why Mrs. Wilcox didn't say anything to us earlier."

For a second, Joey looked as though he was about to cry. But then his expression turned tough. "Don't worry about it," he told Alex. "We can fix it."

Alex started backing away from Joey and shaking his head. He knew exactly what Joey had in mind. There was only one way to fix their predicament. It was the same way they had gotten into this mess in the first place.

Alex and Joey had to ride the Terror-Go-Round again.

*Everyone in Baskerville knows about Jimmy Leeds. In
fact, Adam Riley and his friends have been telling scary
stories about Jimmy for years—stories Adam doesn't
believe. After all, how can anyone believe in a half-human
beast with horns and hooves?*

*Yet the old Leeds house is still standing. And a new Leeds
is living inside it—a Leeds whom Adam and his friends just
can't stand.*

*When Adam and his friend Eugene climb Deadman's
Hill to try to get out of going to J. J. Leeds' birthday party,
they begin to find out that legends aren't always a lie. . . .*

"Let's just get this over with," Adam said impatiently,
taking a step up the drive.

"Sorry, pal." Eugene's feet were still planted on the

"safe" side of the imaginary line. "From here on in, you're on your own. No way I'm climbing Deadman's Hill."

"It's just a driveway," Adam huffed.

"Oh, yeah?" Eugene shot back. "Tell that to the Beast of Baskerville's victims."

"That's just a stupid legend," Adam told him.

"Then how come everyone knows this is the Beast's house?" Eugene demanded.

"*Was* his house," Adam corrected, "two hundred years ago. And no one knows that for sure."

"*Everyone* knows that for sure," Eugene protested. "And everyone knows this is the hill he dragged all his victims up—right before he tore them to shreds and buried them in his well."

"What well?" Adam asked. "Do you see a well on this property?"

"Nooooo," Eugene replied. "But that doesn't mean it's not here."

Adam stared at Eugene. "If you can't *see* the well, then how can it be here?"

"Maybe it's hidden," Eugene suggested.

Adam rolled his eyes. "How the heck do you hide a three-thousand-pound tunnel made out of stone?"

"Who knows?" Eugene answered. "When witches are involved, anything is possible."

"What witches?" Adam asked, exasperated.

"The witches that cursed Elvira," Eugene told him. "The ones that turned Jimmy Leeds into the Beast before he was born."

Elvira Leeds was supposedly the Beast of Baskerville's mother. She was also a witch. According to legend, Elvira

Leeds married a mortal back in the 1800s when the town of Baskerville was first founded. And because she broke the rules of her coven, which stated that witches could marry only warlocks, the other witches cursed her. They turned her husband into a three-headed newt with one eye. Then they put a spell on her unborn child.

When Elvira Leeds finally gave birth to her son, Jimmy, he was only half human. His arms and legs were normal, but the rest of him was beastly.

Two twisted horns shot out of his skull, while two goatlike hooves grew in place of ten human toes. His eyes burned red like flames. And every inch of his body was covered with matted black hair.

Jimmy Leeds was supposedly so hideous that his witch mother tossed him down the well on her property, hoping to be rid of him.

But Jimmy Leeds didn't die. Instead, he grew into the "Beast." Rumor had it that every so often, Jimmy Leeds had climbed out of the well to feed on innocent children.

Some people, like Eugene, believed he still did.

"You know what?" Adam sighed in frustration. "You're a yo-yo. There is no well. And there's no Beast of Baskerville, either. Now are you coming with me or what? Because if you don't come with me, I'll tell J. J. about tent night tonight," he threatened.

"You wouldn't dare!" Eugene turned pale.

"Would too," Adam lied. "And I'll tell everyone else that *you're* the one who told him."

"Tent night" was another reason no one wanted to go to J. J.'s party. All the kids in the neighborhood had been planning to sleep out for weeks. They were all setting up tents in their backyards. Then, when the parents were in bed, the kids were going to sneak out of their yards to play games and hang out.

Needless to say, J. J. wasn't invited.

"I mean it," Adam bluffed. "And I'll tell J. J. you want him to sleep in our tent."

Eugene gave in. "I'll go with you, okay?" he agreed in a panic. "But if something bad happens to us on this hill, I'm blaming you."

"Nothing bad's going to happen to us," Adam assured him.

But Adam was wrong.

Something bad *was* going to happen to them—but not on the hill.

About the Author

A. G. Cascone is the pseudonym of two authors who happen to be sisters . . . "The Twisted Sisters." In addition to *Deadtime Stories*, they have written six books, two horror-movie screenplays, and several pop songs, including one top-ten hit.

If you want to find out more about DEADTIME STORIES or A. G. Cascone, look on the World Wide Web at: http://www.bookwire.com/titles/deadtime/

Also, we'd love to hear from you! You can write to:
    A. G. Cascone
    c/o Troll
    100 Corporate Drive
    Mahwah, NJ 07430

Or you can send e-mail directly to:
agcascone@bookwire.com